SOFTBALL
Surprise

BY JAKE MADDOX

text by Leigh McDonald
illustrated by Katie Wood

STONE ARCH BOOKS
a capstone imprint

Jake Maddox books are published by Stone Arch Books
A Capstone Imprint
1710 Roe Crest Drive
North Mankato, Minnesota 56003
www.capstonepub.com

Library of Congress Cataloging-in-Publication Data

Maddox, Jake, author.
Softball surprise / by Jake Maddox ; text by Leigh McDonald ;
illustrated by Katie Wood.
pages cm. -- (Jake Maddox girl sports stories)
Summary: Jo is disappointed when she is not placed on the Red Angels
in the summer softball league, but when she is offered the chance to
switch teams, Jo has to decide if she will leave her friends and play for the
"winning" team — or win with the Sonics.
ISBN 978-1-4342-4141-2 (hardcover) -- ISBN 978-1-4342-7929-3 (pbk.) --
ISBN 978-1-4342-9285-8 (eBook PDF)
1. Softball--Juvenile fiction. 2. Decision making--Juvenile fiction.
3. Teamwork (Sports)--Juvenile fiction. 4. Friendship--Juvenile
fiction. [1. Softball--Fiction. 2. Decision making--Fiction. 3. Teamwork
(Sports)--Fiction. 4. Friendship--Fiction.] I. McDonald, Leigh, 1979-
author. II. Wood, Katie, 1981- illustrator. III. Title.

PZ7.M25643Soo 2014
[Fic]--dc23

2013028665

Designer: Alison Thiele
Production Specialist: Charmaine Whitman

Printed and bound in the USA.
122016   010185R

TABLE OF CONTENTS

CHAPTER ONE

Team Assignments

"Henry!" Jo Adler exclaimed. "What are you doing? Draw on the paper, not on the baby!"

Henry looked up from where he was drawing on his baby sister's face and giggled. Jo sighed and picked up two-year-old Olivia, who now had green eyebrows drawn above her regular ones. She carried the toddler into the bathroom to wash off the marker.

School had only been out for a week, and Jo was already bored. Babysitting her neighbor's kids was a good way to make some money, but she was ready to do something fun. Something that didn't involve changing diapers.

As she washed Olivia's face, Jo's mind drifted to softball. The summer league started next week, and team assignments would be posted that afternoon.

Last year, Jo had been the center fielder for the Green Hornets. She'd had fun, but the team's name had sounded a lot fiercer than their playing. They'd lost more games than they'd won.

This year, she was hoping to get a spot on the Red Angels. They were the best team in the league every year. They hadn't lost a single game in the past two seasons.

Jo smiled to herself. She couldn't wait to know what it felt like to be on a winning team!

Olivia giggled and squirmed. Most of the marker had come off, so Jo put her down and let her run back into the living room to play with her brother.

Jo tossed the washcloth in the laundry basket and followed after her. "Hey, guys," she said, "want to go outside and play softball?"

"Yeah!" Henry shouted, jumping up from his coloring.

"Ball!" Olivia shouted.

Jo knew they were too little to really play softball, but at least running around outside would be more fun than sitting inside and dreaming about it.

* * *

When she got home later that afternoon, Jo ran upstairs to check the league website.

Unfortunately, the page still said the same thing it had said all week. TEAM ASSIGNMENTS WILL BE POSTED ON JUNE 20TH.

"It is June 20th!" Jo muttered. She went back downstairs to get a snack.

"Hey, sweetie," Jo's mom said, looking up from washing dishes. "Are the teams posted yet?"

"No," Jo said, sighing. "I really hope I get the Red Angels. I want to be on a team that wins!"

"I'm sure it'll be fun no matter what," her mom said. "You'll get to make new friends and play ball either way."

"I know," Jo said. "But it would be really nice to get to do all that and win too."

Her mother laughed. "I know what you mean," she said.

Jo grabbed an apple for a snack and headed back up to her room. She sat down at her computer again to check her email, and suddenly her phone beeped with a text message.

It was from her friend Delia. "WE'RE TEAMMATES!" the message read. "Can't wait for my first season to start!"

The list must be posted! Jo thought.

She clicked back over to the league website. Sure enough, the team rosters were up. Jo quickly scanned for her name and found it — on the Yellow Sonics.

CHAPTER TWO

Making the Best of Things

Jo sighed. She'd really had her heart set on the Red Angels. Still, the news could have been worse. At least the Yellow Sonics were a better team than the Green Hornets.

Reading over the rest of the names on the roster, Jo tried to get over her disappointment. Delia's name was there, along with a couple of other girls she knew. At least it looked like it was going to be a fun team.

Jo clicked on the link for the Red Angels' roster. Most of the girls on the list were the same ones who'd been on the team last year. There were a few other names Jo recognized. They were some of the best players from other league teams.

Jo sighed again and picked up her phone to write Delia back. It was her friend's first time playing in the league. "Want to meet at the park to practice?" she texted.

Delia texted back right away. "Sure!"

Jo got changed and went downstairs again to tell her mother the news. "The teams are up," she said. "I didn't get the Angels. I'm on the Yellow Sonics."

Her mother stopped washing dishes and turned around. "Is that a good team?" she asked.

"It's okay," Jo said, shrugging. "Better than last year, at least. And I know a lot of girls on my team, so that'll be fun. But I still wish I was on the Angels. I guess I'll just have to prove that I'm good enough."

Her mother smiled. "That shouldn't be too hard for you," she said. "Nobody works harder than you do when you put your mind to something."

Jo smiled back. "Thanks, Mom," she said. "Is it okay if I meet Delia at the park to practice? I need to get warmed up for the season, and it would help to play with somebody who can throw the ball farther than two feet. Henry is cute, but he's not much of a pitcher."

"Of course," her mother said. "Just be home by six for dinner."

Delia was waiting for Jo at the park when she arrived. "Ready?" she asked.

Jo nodded. "Definitely," she said.

The girls played catch, starting close together and taking a step back after each successful catch. It was a good way to warm up after many months of not playing softball.

Jo could feel her muscles stretching and flexing. It felt so great that she forgot all about her disappointment over the Angels.

"I'm so glad we get to start playing next week!" she shouted to Delia. "I feel like I've been waiting for this forever!"

"Me too," Delia agreed. "And we're on a team together! This is going to be the best summer ever!"

CHAPTER THREE

First Practice

On Monday, Jo's dad dropped her off at the City Park baseball fields. As they pulled up, she spotted Delia and a couple of other girls from school standing near one of the diamonds.

Jo quickly jumped out of the car and started to jog across the grass to join them.

"Jo!" her dad called after her. "Forgetting something?" He laughed and waved her glove out the window.

Jo shook her head and ran back to retrieve it. "Whoops!" she said.

"Good luck, honey," her dad said, handing her the glove. "And have fun!"

As her dad drove away, Jo turned back to the fields. More girls had gathered around a tall woman wearing a baseball hat and a yellow jacket.

When she reached the group, Jo saw a big box of yellow T-shirts sitting on the grass. "Are those our team uniforms?" she asked.

The woman in the baseball hat smiled at her. "Yes," she said, "but let's wait for everyone to get here before handing them out. I'm Coach Johnson. What's your name?"

"Jo Adler," Jo replied.

The coach made a checkmark on the clipboard she was holding. "Welcome, Jo," she said. "You played with the league last year, right?"

Jo nodded. "I was center fielder for the Green Hornets. I'd really like to move to the infield this year, though," she said.

"I'll keep that in mind," the coach told her, smiling and making a note.

A few more girls walked up, and the coach moved away to take down their names.

"Okay!" Coach Johnson announced a moment later. "If I could have everyone's attention, please. I think we're all here, so welcome to the Yellow Sonics!"

Everyone clapped. "Yay!" a couple of girls shouted.

Jo raised her hand. "Do we have our schedule yet?" she asked.

"We'll have practice every Monday, and every Wednesday will be game day," Coach Johnson replied with a smile. "Any other questions?"

Nobody said anything, so the coach picked up a big box and started handing out shirts. The words "Yellow Sonics" were printed across the front of the T-shirts. Al's Hardware, the local business sponsoring their team this year, was written across the back.

"It's time to play ball! We'll start with some warm-ups," the coach said. "Then we'll move into fielding exercises. I'll assign positions after I've had a chance to see everyone play."

Jo pulled her T-shirt on over the tank top she'd been wearing and headed out toward the middle of the field. She and Delia tossed a ball back and forth for a few minutes to warm up.

"Let's practice fielding," Coach Johnson called from her position near home plate. She picked up a bat and began hitting balls into the outfield.

Jo was determined to make a good impression. Every time a ball came toward her, she hustled after it. She snagged fly balls out of the air and kept her glove low to the ground to scoop up ground balls.

After thirty minutes of fielding practice, Coach Johnson called, "Bring it in, girls! Everybody gather around to hear your positions."

Coach Johnson started reading off positions. "Jo Adler, second base," she said.

Jo grinned happily. Second base was a great position.

"Delia Jones, right field," the coach continued.

Jo heard Delia sigh. Right field was a little boring, since few balls ended up getting hit there.

Jo caught up to her friend as they walked toward the parking lot. "Don't worry, Delia," she said. "I'll practice with you anytime you want! You won't be in right field forever."

"Thanks, Jo," Delia said, perking up a little. "Today was fun either way."

"Yeah!" Jo said, bumping Delia with her hip. "And we're just getting started."

CHAPTER FOUR

Luck Doesn't Last

The Yellow Sonics had their first game the following week. They were playing the Blue Sharks. Jo was so excited and nervous that she bounced in her seat the whole way to the park.

The Sonics were up to bat first. Jo took a seat on the team's bench and cheered on her teammates. Lucy, the first baseman, was up first. She let a couple of balls go by without swinging.

"Good eye!" Jo called out.

Lucy gripped her bat and waited for the next pitch. It came straight across the plate. Lucy swung but missed.

"Strike!" the umpire called.

The pitcher threw the next ball right down the middle of the plate again. This time Lucy swung and connected. The ball went sailing way out into center field.

Lucy took off running. She made it all the way to second base before the center fielder chased the ball down and threw it back to the infield.

Jo and the rest of the Sonics jumped up and down, cheering. What a great start!

Their luck didn't last, though. The next two batters both struck out, and Lucy was stuck waiting on second base.

With two outs, Jo was up to bat. She couldn't let Lucy's leadoff double go to waste! She walked up to the plate slowly, taking a deep breath to clear her mind. Then she got into position, looked at the pitcher, and waited.

The first pitch came toward the plate, and just as it reached her, Jo swung. There was a loud crack as the bat connected with the ball. It sailed out over the infield, and Jo took off running as fast as she could down the first-base line.

As she reached first base, Jo saw the left fielder out of the corner of her eye, scooping the ball up from the ground. Jo stopped where she was and heard loud cheering from the bench. She turned just in time to see Lucy crossing home plate, scoring the team's first run.

Unfortunately, the next girl up to the plate struck out, which meant the Sharks were up to bat. Jo headed back to the bench to grab her glove and got a few high fives on the way.

The Sonics had gotten off to a great start, but things went downhill from there. The second Sharks' player up to bat hit a pop fly into right field, straight to Delia. She tried to get under the ball to catch it, but slipped and fumbled the ball. The runner made it all the way to third base before Delia recovered.

Several more bad innings followed. The Sonics kept striking out, and their fielding errors gave the Sharks a chance to score more runs. By the time they were in the bottom of the ninth inning, the score was 4-1 Sharks.

After the game, the two teams shook hands, and Jo gathered her equipment. She was walking back to the parking lot when she heard loud cheering from a nearby field.

Jo turned and saw that the Angels had just finished their opening game too. The whole team was jumping up and down, giving each other high fives and hugs. The scoreboard read 10-0.

Jo sighed in frustration. *Must be nice to be on a winning team*, she thought. *Not that I'd know.*

CHAPTER FIVE

Practice Makes Perfect

A week later, Jo and Delia were back in the park practicing fielding techniques. They'd been running drills all afternoon on top of the practice they'd had that morning. Jo was determined to fix the mistakes from their first game.

"Remember, don't reach up for the ball until the last moment," Jo said. She tossed another ball in Delia's direction, this one high in the air.

Delia positioned herself under the falling ball. Her fielding skills were improving, and she seemed more confident than she had been during the first game.

"Awesome!" Jo called as Delia reached up with two hands and caught the ball securely in her baseball glove. "I think you've got it!"

Delia grinned and jogged over to where Jo stood. "I'm feeling a lot better now," she said. "Thanks for practicing with me!"

"That's what teammates are for," Jo said.

* * *

At practice on Monday, the coach complimented Delia on her improved fielding. And when they showed up for the game on Wednesday, her name was listed for center field instead of right.

Jo gave her a high five. "I knew you wouldn't be picking clover in right field for long!" she told her friend.

The first few innings were tight, with both teams scoring a single run. Delia caught a few pop flies and tossed them back into the infield with ease.

Then in the sixth inning, Jo hit the first triple of the season, scoring two runs. Her teammates cheered for her happily. Jo jogged around the bases, grinning from ear to ear.

The next two players up to bat both hit singles, scoring another run before the inning was out. But their energy and good luck seemed to rub off on the other team too. They started driving hits past the Sonics and into the outfield.

Even though Jo made every play that came her way, it wasn't enough to save the game. In the end, the score was 5-4. The Sonics had lost again.

* * *

At dinner that night, Jo picked at her grilled chicken.

"What's wrong, honey?" her mom finally asked. "You don't seem like yourself tonight."

"I don't know, Mom," Jo said. She sighed and pushed her food around her plate. "I'm playing better than ever, but our team keeps losing. It's really frustrating."

Her mom reached over and squeezed her arm. "I know it makes you sad to lose, but I hope you know that I'm really proud of you. You're doing so well out there."

"It just doesn't seem like enough," Jo muttered.

"I'm sure your coach knows how hard you're working," her mom said. "And you're helping your teammates get better too! That's real sportsmanship."

"Thanks, Mom," Jo said. "I just wish I was on a team where it made a difference!"

"Well," her mom said, "just keep doing what you're doing. I know those wins will start to come your way."

CHAPTER SIX

The Truth Comes Out

"Can we go to the library, Jo? Can we, can we?" Henry begged.

Jo was babysitting again, and going to the library sounded like a great way to pass some time.

"Olivia, what do you think?" she asked the toddler cheerfully. "Books?"

Olivia hopped up and down. "Books!" she shouted.

"Okay, guys, into the wagon!" Jo said, heading for the front door.

She loaded the kids into their wagon and pulled them along the sidewalk. The library was only a few blocks away, near the park where she and Delia went to practice.

As they passed the park, Jo noticed a couple of players from the Red Angels tossing a ball around in the field.

Jo felt a twinge of jealousy, but before she could give it too much thought, they'd reached the library doors. The kids quickly climbed out of the wagon. Henry tugged the big glass doors open, and they all filed inside.

After a few minutes of reading, Olivia looked up from the pile of picture books and made a face at Jo. "Need potty," she said.

Jo sighed. "Okay, Henry, you stay here while I take your sister to the bathroom," she said.

She took Olivia to the bathroom and helped her into a stall. The bathroom door squeaked open and thumped shut again.

"I mean, it's almost too easy," a voice said. "You'd think they'd at least leave some decent players on the other teams so we could have a real game once in a while."

"Well, when your dad runs the league, I guess you get whatever coach and teammates you want!" another voice said. "Besides, who cares? Wins are wins."

The water ran for a minute and then stopped. "Yeah, for real," the first voice said. "I'm not saying I want to be stuck on the Devils or anything. Ugh."

"All done!" Olivia announced loudly.

The voices immediately stopped, and the door squeaked open and shut again.

Jo realized she was holding her breath, and let it out slowly.

Those must have been the Red Angels from the park! she thought as she helped Olivia to the sink.

She couldn't believe it. The Red Angels weren't getting all those wins because they worked harder than the other teams. They were taking the best players and coaches for themselves.

No wonder no one can beat them, Jo thought angrily.

As much as Jo wanted to win, she wanted to earn it. What the Angels were doing almost sounded like . . . cheating.

CHAPTER SEVEN

Too Good to Refuse?

The following Wednesday, Jo waited on second base, watching the batter carefully. The Sonics were playing the Angels, and they were down by three runs. Jo was really hoping the double she'd just hit would turn into a run.

Crack! The bat connected with the ball, and Jo took off running as fast as she could. As she touched third base, she saw that the ball had been hit into right field. The fielder was just scooping it up.

Jo rounded third and charged toward home plate. She heard the ball smack into the catcher's glove half a second after her foot touched the plate.

Score! Her teammates went crazy. They were still down two runs, but at least now they were on the board.

Jo took a seat on the bench, breathing hard and grinning. The next batter took her place at the plate and stared at the pitcher.

The first pitch looked like a ball, but the umpire called, "Strike!" The rest of the Sonics groaned.

"It's okay, just stay focused!" the coach called.

Lucy, the Sonic on first base, shifted nervously. She was ready to run as soon as the pitcher released the ball.

The next pitch sailed across the plate, and the batter swung at it hard. It bounced oddly off the bat and sailed over the pitcher's head toward second base.

Lucy was already running, and the second baseman and shortstop both moved toward the ball. There was a moment of confusion over who should grab it.

As Lucy reached the base, the Angels' shortstop was just reaching out for the ball. The two girls collided.

Jo heard a sharp cry, and then the Angels' shortstop crumpled to the ground, clutching her hand. Both coaches went running toward her.

After a few minutes, Lucy and the Sonics' coach came slowly back to the bench. Lucy's eyes were a little red, like she'd been crying.

"The shortstop broke her finger," the coach told them. "She'll be fine, but we're going to stop the game for today. We'll schedule a rematch later."

The girls all looked worried and upset. Delia put her arm around Lucy.

"It was an accident," the coach assured her. "We try to be as careful as we can when we play, but sometimes these things happen. It's nobody's fault. Don't worry — the doctors will get her fixed up in no time."

* * *

Later that night, Jo was reading in her room when her phone rang. She looked at the screen but didn't recognize the number.

"Hello?" Jo answered curiously.

"Is this Josephine Adler?" a woman's voice asked.

"Yes, it is. Who's calling?" Jo asked.

"This is Coach Sanderson from the Red Angels," the voice said.

Jo sat back on her bed, shocked. *Why would the Angels' coach be calling me?* she wondered.

She realized after a moment that she hadn't said anything, and the coach was waiting.

"Um, what can I do for you?" Jo finally said.

"I know you saw what happened to our shortstop at the game today," the coach said. "I just heard from her, and it looks like she'll be out for the rest of the season. Your name came up as a possible replacement. How would you like to be a Red Angel, Josephine?"

Jo's heart pounded in her chest. She'd wanted to be a Red Angel for so long. But now that the chance was finally here, she wasn't sure it was what she wanted anymore.

Especially after what I heard those girls say about how the Angels got all those wins, Jo thought.

"Um, thank you," Jo said to the coach. "Do I need to decide right now, or can I think about it?"

"Oh," the coach said, sounding surprised. "Well, I can certainly give you a little time to think it over. Please call me by this weekend and let me know what you decide. We have a game next week, and I'd like to get our new player up to speed as soon as possible."

"Okay," Jo said. "Thanks again. I'll let you know."

She hung up the phone and flopped back on her bed. Jo's mind was racing, but all her thoughts added up to one big question: *What am I going to do?*

CHAPTER EIGHT

Choosing the Right Team

The Angels' next practice was Friday, so Jo talked Delia into coming with her to watch. They rode the bus down to City Park after school. Jo hadn't told Delia that the Angels had asked her to play for them, just that she wanted to see how they practiced.

Which is true, Jo thought. *It's not like I'm lying.*

"Maybe we can pick up some tips," Delia suggested.

The two girls walked over to the field nervously. They chose a spot behind some parents so they wouldn't be noticed.

The Angels practiced batting and fielding for a long time. They were very serious and got through way more drills than the Sonics usually did. It helped that all of the players seemed practically perfect.

Jo and Delia took note of the drills they hadn't tried before. After a while, they took the bus back to their neighborhood.

"Maybe we should call some of the other girls and see if they want to practice," Jo suggested on the way. "We can try out some of the drills we saw."

"Great idea!" Delia agreed. She pulled out her phone and started calling some of their teammates.

By the time they reached the park, four other girls were waiting.

Jo and Delia shared what they'd learned at the Angels' practice, and the girls got busy. They spent the most time on a drill designed to improve their reaction time.

The players all took turns hitting balls into the field where the other girls quickly threw them back. Then the batter caught the ball and hit it back again as quickly as possible.

It took some of the girls a while to catch onto some of the more complicated drills, but everyone had a lot of fun.

By the time her last teammate had left to go home for dinner, Jo knew what she had to do. She walked home, feeling nervous but happy, and went straight to her room.

Jo picked up the phone and dialed Coach Sanderson's number. The phone rang twice, and she heard a click.

"Hello?" the coach said.

"Hello, Coach Sanderson?" Jo said politely. "This is Jo Adler. You called me about joining the Angels."

"Oh, yes, hello, Jo," the coach replied. "I saw that you came to our practice today. Are you ready to join the Angels? I can get you a —"

Jo interrupted, not wanting to waste any time. "I've decided I'm going to stay on the Sonics," she said. "Thank you for the offer, but I'm happy with my team. And I want to help them win."

"Oh, I see," the coach said. "Well, that's very nice of you, Jo. Are you sure?"

"Very sure," Jo said.

"I guess I'll see you on the field, then. Thanks for letting me know," the coach said.

Jo felt like a huge weight had been lifted from her shoulders. She let out a sigh of relief and headed downstairs.

"Hey, Mom!" she called. "What's for dinner?"

CHAPTER NINE

All Tied Up

Jo stared out the window of her dad's car as they drove toward the softball field, eyeing the clouds for any sign of rain. Things were looking up lately. A lot of the girls were still meeting up in the afternoons to practice in the park, and the Sonics had won three of their past four games.

Today was their rematch against the Red Angels, and Jo couldn't decide whether she was more nervous or excited.

I can't take another delay, she thought as they drove.

Luckily, the clouds held off, and the game started on time. The Red Angels were up to bat first. They scored a run in the first inning, but the Sonics' extra practice paid off and they held them there.

Nobody managed to score for the next seven innings, though. Lucy hit a double in the third inning but was left stranded on base. Delia hit a grounder to third in the fifth inning, but she was tagged out while running after the next batter's hit went straight to the Angels' center fielder.

Jo was starting to get nervous. Even if they fielded perfectly for the rest of the game, the Angels were still on the scoreboard, and the Sonics were not.

We have to get some runs on the board, she thought.

In the eighth inning, Jo was up to bat. There was one out and no one on base. She took a deep breath and forced herself not to think about the score, the Angels, or anything else. Nothing but the pitch coming toward her.

The pitcher let the ball fly. It sailed to the outside of the plate.

"Ball!" the umpire called.

Jo shifted her stance and waited. The next pitch came straight down the middle, a little on the low side, but hard and fast.

Jo saw it arc perfectly, almost like it was in slow motion. With one smooth swing, she brought the bat around and hit the ball with a satisfying *CRACK!*

The ball sailed over the outfield as Jo took off running. The Angels' outfielders fell back and back until they'd hit the fence.

Did I really just hit a home run? Jo thought as she raced around the bases.

Back at the bench, her teammates were going crazy. The Sonics jumped up and down, shouting her name at the top of their lungs and cheering.

Jo jogged past home plate and over to her team, who mobbed her with high fives and hugs.

"Nice work, Jo," her coach congratulated her. She let the team celebrate for a moment. "Okay, girls, have a seat. We still have another inning to go. And the Angels aren't going to make it easy for you. We all need to stay focused."

"Yes, coach," the girls said. They sat back down on the bench, but grinned at Jo again when the coach turned away.

The next two Sonics at bat struck out, and then the Angels were up to bat again. Jo knew they were just as determined to win as the Sonics.

We can't afford to make any mistakes, she thought determinedly.

The Sonics' pitcher managed to strike out the first Angel up to bat. Unfortunately, the second batter hit a ball into left field for a single.

The next batter sent a fly ball soaring into center field. Delia caught it easily for the out, but the runner on base made it all the way to second before she could throw the ball in to Jo.

The next at-bat was a big one. If the batter got a hit, chances were good that the Angels would score.

The Sonics would be down a run once again. And this time, they'd only have one more chance to score.

The Sonics' pitcher let the ball fly, and the batter hit it hard. The ball flew straight toward first base, where Lucy was ready and waiting. She caught it with a loud *smack!*

The Sonics all breathed a quick sigh of relief. Then they headed toward their bench for their final at-bat, the score still tied 1-1.

CHAPTER TEN

The Final Inning

Delia was up to bat first. She walked up to the plate with a focused look on her face. The first pitch came straight across the plate, and she hit a nice grounder toward third base.

Jessie Smith, the Sonics' left fielder, was up next. She hit a fly ball into right field, sending the Angels' outfielders racing after it. Delia managed to make it to third base, while Jessie waited at first.

The next batter was Elizabeth, the Sonics' shortstop. She smacked the ball straight back toward the pitcher's mound, but the ball made it to first base before she did. Luckily Jessie made it to second base on her hit, while Delia stayed at third.

With two runners on base, Lucy stepped up to the plate. The first two pitches were balls. Lucy got a piece of the third pitch, but it popped straight up in the air. Foul ball, and strike one.

Finally, on the fourth pitch, Lucy got a solid hit. The ball flew straight up the first-base line. The first baseman caught it, tagging Lucy out.

But as Lucy was tagged out, Delia took off from third base and raced for home. She charged across the plate, scoring the winning run.

The Sonics on the bench went crazy. They'd done it! It was the first win against the Angels in three seasons, and they'd done it together.

* * *

After their big win, Coach Johnson took the whole team out for ice cream to celebrate.

"I think this is the best ice cream I've ever had in my life," Jo said around a mouthful of fudge ripple.

"That's because it tastes like victory!" Delia told her, laughing.

Coach Johnson smiled. "You guys earned it," she said proudly. "I've never seen a team work as hard as all of you did this season. The Yellow Sonics are the team to beat!"

"Well," Lucy said, "we aren't quite the Red Angels. . . ."

"Exactly," Jo said firmly. "We weren't given a team of winners — we made it ourselves!"

"I don't know about you guys," Lucy added, "but I'm still going to the park whenever I can."

"Me too," several of the girls agreed.

Delia linked her arm through Jo's, and both girls smiled.

"Now this is the best summer ever!" Jo said.

AUTHOR BIO

Leigh McDonald loves books! Whether she is writing them, reading them, editing them, or designing their covers, books are what she does best. She lives in a colorful bungalow in Tucson, Arizona, with her husband, Porter, her daughter, Adair, and two big, crazy dogs, Roscoe! and Rosie.

ILLUSTRATOR BIO

Katie Wood fell in love with drawing when she was very small. Since graduating from Loughborough University School of Art and Design in 2004, she has been living her dream working as a freelance illustrator. From her studio in Leicester, England, she creates bright and lively illustrations for books and magazines all over the world.

GLOSSARY

equipment (i-KWIP-muhnt) — the tools, machines, and gear needed for a particular purpose

fierce (FIHRSS) — violent or dangerous; very strong or extreme

impression (im-PRESH-uhn) — an idea or a feeling

infield (IN-feeld) — in baseball, the area enclosed by home plate and the bases

league (LEEG) — a group of people with a common interest or activity, such as a group of sports teams or a political organization

outfield (OUT-feeld) — the area of a baseball field between the foul lines and beyond the infield

retrieve (ri-TREEV) — to get or bring something back

DISCUSSION QUESTIONS

1. Do you think what the Red Angels were doing was fair? Talk about why or why not.

2. Was Jo right to be disappointed when she found out which softball team she was on? How would you have felt? Discuss your opinion.

3. Did Jo make the right choice to stick with her team? Or should she have joined the Red Angels when she had the chance? Talk about your opinion.

WRITING PROMPTS

1. Write a paragraph about what you would have done when you found out about the Red Angels if you were in Jo's shoes.

2. Which softball position would you like to play? Write a paragraph explaining your choice.

3. Imagine you are the coach of the Red Angels. Write a paragraph about how you would react to Jo's decision.

MORE ABOUT SOFTBALL

During a softball game, there are nine players on the field at a time, each of whom has a different role. Which position is right for you? Read on to learn more about each one.

- **Pitcher** — throws the ball from the pitcher's mound to home plate, attempting to strike the batter out.

- **Catcher** — stays crouched behind home plate to signal and receive pitches; the catcher also throws balls to other bases to throw out runners.

- **First baseman** — stands at first base and receives throws from other defensive players in order to quickly tag runners out; usually involved in every play.

- **Second baseman** — plays in the gap between the first baseman and second base. If a ball is hit to the left side of the field, this player covers second base; if it goes right, the player fields the ball, covers first, or backs up another fielder.

- **Shortstop** — fields all balls that fall between the second and third bases; this player also helps cover second base and third base and throws to the catcher.

- **Third baseman** — covers hits to third base and often throws to the catcher to throw out runners at home plate.

- **Outfielders** — these are considered defensive positions and are responsible for catching fly balls and returning long hits to the infield. There are three outfielders: the left fielder, center fielder, and right fielder.

THE FUN DOESN'T STOP HERE!

Discover more:

VIDEOS & CONTESTS
GAMES & PUZZLES
HEROES & VILLAINS
AUTHORS & ILLUSTRATORS

www.capstonekids.com

Find cool websites and more books just like this one at **www.facthound.com**.

Just type in the book I.D.

9781434241412

and you're ready to go!